4/10

READ ALL THE BOOKS

In The

New MATT CHRISTOPHER Sports Library!

BASEBALL FLYHAWK
978-1-59953-354-4

THE BASKET COUNTS
978-1-59953-212-7

CATCH THAT PASS
978-1-59953-105-2

CENTER COURT STING
978-1-59953-106-9

THE COMEBACK CHALLENGE
978-1-59953-211-0

DIRT BIKE RACER
978-1-59953-113-7

DIRT BIKE RUNAWAY
978-1-59953-215-8

THE GREAT QUARTERBACK SWITCH
978-1-59953-216-5

THE HOCKEY MACHINE
978-1-59953-214-1

ICE MAGIC
978-1-59953-112-0

THE KID WHO ONLY HIT HOMERS
978-1-59953-107-6

LACROSSE FACE-OFF
978-1-59953-355-1

LONG-ARM QUARTERBACK
978-1-59953-114-4

MOUNTAIN BIKE MANIA
978-1-59953-108-3

POWER PITCHER
978-1-59953-356-8

RETURN OF THE HOME RUN KID
978-1-59953-213-4

SHOOT FOR THE HOOP
978-1-59953-357-5

SKATEBOARD TOUGH
978-1-59953-115-1

SNOWBOARD MAVERICK
978-1-59953-116-8

SNOWBOARD SHOWDOWN
978-1-59953-109-0

SOCCER HALFBACK
978-1-59953-110-6

SOCCER SCOOP
978-1-59953-117-5

THE TEAM THAT COULDN'T LOSE
978-1-59953-358-2

TOUGH TO TACKLE
978-1-59953-359-9

The New

Sports Library

THE TEAM THAT
COULDN'T
LOSE

NORWOOD HOUSE PRESS

CHICAGO, ILLINOIS

Norwood House Press
P.O. Box 316598
Chicago, Illinois 60631

For information regarding Norwood House Press, please visit our website
at: www.norwoodhousepress.com or call 866-565-2900.

This library edition was published in 2010.

Library of Congress Cataloging-in-Publication Data:
Christopher, Matt.
  The team that couldn't lose / by Matt Christopher.
    p. cm. — (The new Matt Christopher sports library)
  Summary: A young, inexperienced football team discovers that its
beginner's luck is due to a series of mysterious but successful plays
anonymously sent to the coach.
  ISBN-13: 978-1-59953-358-2 (library edition : alk. paper)
  ISBN-10: 1-59953-358-8 (library edition : alk. paper)
  (1. Football—Fiction.) I. Title. II. Title: Team that could not lose.
  PZ7.C458Te 2010
  (Fic)—dc22
                            2009038996

Manufactured in the United States of America in
North Mankato, Minnesota.
                            N145—012010

To

Coach Stan Sobus

★ ★

THE TEAM THAT COULDN'T LOSE

All right, men!" yelled Coach Tom Kash. "Let's try that play again! You guys on defense, charge in there! Your job is to try to stop Chip from throwing the ball!"

Chip Chase wiped his brow with the sleeve of his jersey and got into position again behind center Toots Egan. It was a muggy day. The Cayugans had been practicing for almost an hour and were getting very tired.

They needed practice, though. They needed it badly. They had scrimmaged the

Duckbills last Saturday and were slaughtered 28–0. And their first league game was this coming Saturday, just five days away.

It was the rain that had caused all the trouble. It had rained so much during the past two weeks that the team couldn't get together enough for practice. And the Cayugans simply had to practice as much as they possibly could. They had twenty-one players on the roster, but too many of them knew too little about football. Chip, Splash Tuttle, and Spencer Keel were the only three who had played football at least two years. The other guys had played only one year, or not even that.

"Down!" yelled Chip.

The linemen and the backfield men got down instantly, left arms balanced on their left knees, right hands pressed against the short-cropped grass.

"One! Two! Three! Hip!"

Toots Egan snapped the ball. Chip took it, turned, faked a handoff to fullback Spencer Keel, then faded back. He saw Splash running down the left side of the park, a defenseman about two yards behind him.

Chip reared back with both hands on the ball because he couldn't grip it with one hand. His fingers were too short.

Three guys broke through the line and charged at him. He removed his left hand from the ball, then heaved the ball in the direction of Splash Tuttle.

It was a near-perfect throw, arcing down just ahead of Splash. Splash caught it with both hands and ran hard down the field. The man covering him couldn't get close enough to touch him. If this were a real game, it would've been a touchdown.

It was the best play of the three that Coach Tom Kash had taught them. They were all simple plays. The coach didn't think they'd be able to perform more difficult ones.

Chip heard a shout from the sideline. "Nice pass, Chip! Good arm!"

That was Danny Livermore, the team's manager. He was slim and short and two years younger than Chip. He wasn't eligible to play in the league yet, but he was allowed to help out as manager.

Chip rolled his eyes. That kid! he thought. Why does he always have to try to be my best friend?

It wasn't that Chip didn't like the little guy. But Danny's hero worship of Chip was embarrassing sometimes. That wouldn't have been so bad, but Danny kept hoping to get Chip interested in his hobbies. Hobbies like collecting butterflies and flowers, and going to flea markets and garage sales. He was always carrying around this crazy notebook with things pasted in it or written down.

Chip just wasn't keen on any of that stuff — or on spending more time with Danny.

Chip was sure that Danny could become just about anything he wanted to when he grew up. He was that smart. He didn't look it, but he was. He was a whiz at math and wrote compositions more easily than any kid in Chip's grade. He was adventurous, too, for someone his size. He had gone alone into the woods two or three times to collect leaves. There was a swamp in the middle of the woods, but that didn't faze Danny.

If only he didn't try so hard, thought Chip.

"Okay, fellas," Coach Tom Kash said. "Get around me a minute. "Got something to tell you."

Beside him stood Phil Wayne, his assistant coach. Phil was a young man, no older than twenty-two, with short, dark hair. Although he was well liked, he really knew very little about football.

"Boys," Tom Kash said after the team had assembled in front of him, "I don't know whether you've heard this, but some of us at the computer plant have been transferred to other parts of the country. I regret to say that I am one of them."

Chip stared at him.

"This is my last day with you," the coach continued. "Phil Wayne will be your head coach from now on. I have asked Adam Quigley, Firehose's dad, to assist him, and he says he'll be glad to. Phil played football for two years in high school, and so did Mr. Quigley. I don't expect that you'll win every game in the league, but with a lot of hard work and cooperation — and if you listen to Mr. Wayne and Mr. Quigley — I don't see why you can't win at least a couple."

He smiled. "You're only playing six games, so that would be thirty-three and one-third percent. Not a bad average, really, considering that most of you ballplayers are about as green as Phil's sweatshirt."

"My only request now is that you call me Coach or Phil, not Mr. Wayne," Phil said. "Mr. Wayne is my father!" The boys laughed. Chip saw Phil grin at Mr. Kash.

"You've learned three plays fairly well," said Mr. Kash. "It's too bad that we've had so much rain. I think we would've had a better team. Practice every day from now on — with Fridays off as rest days." He smiled. "Well, boys, this is it. It's been a lot of fun. I'm awfully sorry I can't be with you any longer. I love football. I love to coach it, especially to a bunch of hardworking boys like you. Maybe I'll stop and see you play one of these days. Good luck!"

Some of the boys stood staring at him as if his words had glued them to the ground. Others ran up to him and shook his hand and told him how much they'd miss him.

Chip was one of those who couldn't move. Finally, he did. He went up to Mr. Kash and shook his hand and said that he was sorry to see him go.

Chip turned away, feeling as blue as anyone could feel. With Phil Wayne as head coach and Mr. Quigley as assistant coach, he couldn't see how the Cayugans could possibly win a game. As a matter of fact, he predicted that the Cayugans would lose every single one of them.

Chip didn't care about going to practice on Tuesday. With Mr. Kash gone, the team would be nothing. Neither Phil Wayne nor Mr. Quigley knew enough about football to coach a team. All the coaches in the league were supposed to have the qualifications of knowing football and how to coach, but neither Phil nor Mr. Quigley had.

The trouble was that there weren't enough men in town who could qualify. Those who could already had teams to coach, except Bart Franks, the former college football star of Notre Dame. He wasn't able to coach, though, because he was a salesman and on the road most of the time.

Chip wished his father could coach. But Mr. Chase had never played football. He knew even less about it than Phil Wayne did. He enjoyed the game, though. He had seen all the games last year, and he enjoyed watching the pro games on TV.

Anyway, Chip's dad was plenty busy with other things. He and Mrs. Chase were co-presidents of the PTA. He was also secretary of the Lions Club and chairman of a tool designers' organization. He couldn't find time to coach a football team even if he knew how.

Chip attended practice only because he didn't want to let Phil Wayne or Mr. Quigley down. He went over to get Splash Tuttle, and the two of them walked together to the park.

"Hi, Chip! Hi, Splash!" Danny Livermore called, cracking a wide grin.

Chip gave a half-wave.

"What a nut," Splash muttered. "Smiles no matter if we lose every game in the league."

Phil came over.

"Hi, fellas," he said. "Been waiting for you. I want the backfield men to drill on pass plays and line plunges, so put on your helmets and let's get into our positions." He turned and yelled to the players running around on the field, throwing and catching footballs. Nine players broke away from the group and came trotting forward.

Two of them were fullback Spencer Keel and right halfback Gordie Poole. The other seven were linemen. Chip saw Mr. Quigley working with a group near the side of the field. He saw the quarterback fumble a pass from center, then stumble all over himself trying to pick it up.

Chip looked away, shaking his head. What a sad-looking bunch *they* were!

"Line up, men," Phil ordered. He named off the linemen, then glanced over the men in the backfield. Mr. Kash had taught the backfield men the basic formation, so the boys got into their positions without difficulty.

Phil looked up from his notebook. "Can you remember what Play Forty-two is?" he asked.

"Yes," answered Chip. "I hand off the ball to Spence and he takes off between left guard and center."

Phil nodded. "Right. Okay, let's try it."

They tried it — again and again. Since Mr. Kash had taught them the play, they must have run it a million times. It was the same with the other plays in which Spence carried the ball. He played fullback because he was the biggest and hardest to bring down. But that didn't mean that the play was successful each time. It wasn't.

They tried the pass plays, which were a sad thing, too. Chip was the only member of the team who could throw a football well. Therefore only he did the passing.

He threw a long one down the left side of the field to the left end and then down the right side of the field to the right end, and both times the receivers missed the ball. Phil had them try the play until both ends caught the passes thrown to them. By that time Chip's arm was beginning to ache. Boy, what a couple of crummy ends, he thought.

Phil exchanged players on the line with the group being coached by Mr. Quigley, then had the two squads scrimmage against each other. Since there were only twenty-one players on the Cayugans team, Mr. Quigley had to be satisfied with ten men. Both squads were given opportunities to carry the ball. Chip noticed that the squad he was on wasn't much good, but the other squad was even worse.

He was glad when Phil finally shouted, "Okay, boys! That's it for tonight! See you tomorrow!"

"Maybe," Chip heard Splash say. "Oh, I guess I'll be here," Splash added as he met Chip's eyes.

Chip didn't say it, but that was how he felt about it, too.

3

When five-thirty rolled around on Wednesday and Chip didn't put on his uniform, his mom looked at him questioningly. "Isn't there football practice tonight, Chip?" she asked.

"Yes, but —" Chip hated to tell her.

"But, what?"

"Well, Mr. Kash is gone, and Phil Wayne and Mr. Quigley are coaching us. Those guys don't know anything about football. I don't want to be on a team that's going to be skinned every game."

"Oh? Don't you think you should give Mr.

Wayne and Mr. Quigley a chance to see what they can do?"

"I've seen what Phil can do. And I don't think Mr. Quigley can do any better."

He knew that was a poor attitude to take. He expected his mom to tell him so. But she only looked at him silently. She didn't have to tell him.

He stuck to his decision. He wasn't going to practice — today, tomorrow, nor any other time. He would tell Phil Wayne he had quit the team as soon as he saw him. By that time, he'd think of a good reason to give Phil. He would have to return the uniform to Phil, too.

Mr. Chase came home a few minutes before six. He, too, wondered why Chip hadn't gone to football practice. Chip told him the same thing he had told his mom. Chip expected his dad to say that it was a poor attitude to take. But he didn't. He probably figured that Chip was old enough now to know that it was a poor attitude without telling him.

After dinner Chip went to his room and started on his homework. There was a page of math he had to do, and a short composition to write. He did the first two math problems all right, then encountered trouble. It wasn't the math problem. It was a thought that kept nagging at his mind: Phil Wayne, Mr. Quigley, and the Cayugans. He could see them all at the field without him. He wondered who was working out at quarterback. Bill Perrett? Luther Otis?

He kept pushing the football thoughts out of his mind. But they kept coming back. He finally finished the math problems, then started on his composition. That was even worse. He wrote a full page, saw the many words he had scratched out on it, then crumbled up the paper, threw it into a wastebasket, and started another. It was almost bedtime when he had finished a composition he was satisfied with.

Thursday at school, the boys wanted to know where he had been last night. "Home," he said. "I didn't feel well." He didn't have to tell them the truth, did he?

"Phil Wayne and Mr. Quigley taught us a new play," said Splash. "It's real tough."

"I bet," said Chip. Real tough. How could Phil Wayne and Mr. Quigley teach them a real tough play when all they knew were the plays Mr. Kash had taught them?

Now and then throughout the day, the thought of missing football practice popped into Chip's mind. What did Splash mean when he said that Phil Wayne and Mr. Quigley were teaching the team a new play? A real tough new play?

It was the longest school day Chip had

lived through in a long time. He was glad when it was over. At home, he came out of his room at a quarter after five, wearing his football uniform. His mom looked at him with a pleased glint in her eyes. "We'll hold up supper for you," she said.

The whole Cayugans team seemed glad to see him. "You oughta see the new play Phil and Mr. Quigley are teaching us," Chazz Davis said, excitedly. "It's great!"

Chip smiled. It sure was good to be at practice, no matter how poor the Cayugans were!

"Chip Chase," said Phil Wayne, "you weren't here last evening, so you missed out on our first practice of a new play. Take your quarterback position. Luther, you just stand aside and keep your ears open. First team, get into positions for Play One."

The men promptly moved into their positions. Then Phil Wayne explained in detail the job each man had to do, just as he must have done yesterday. Left end Hans Lodder and left tackle Jim Kolar were to run ahead and to the right across the field to run interference for the ballcarrier. Left guard Marty Tripp and center Toots Egan were to block the right linebackers. Right guard Firehose Quigley was to block the left linebacker. Right tackle Chazz Davis and right end Tracy Tinker had men to block, too.

The other big job was in the backfield. Chip Chase, playing quarterback, would get the pass from center, fake a handoff to right halfback Gordie Poole, then toss a lateral to Splash Tuttle, who would be running from his left halfback position toward and then around right end. Fullback Spencer Keel's job was to take out the defensive end.

They tried the play. They went over it again and again and again. Chip was amazed and pleased. The play was tough, just as

Splash had said. But it looked like a real good one. Chip's opinion of Phil Wayne slowly began to change.

"We need a strong defense," Phil told the team. "You boys on the line, bust through. Bring down that ballcarrier. Stop that pass. Linebackers, watch every play closely. Stop those rushes. Intercept those passes. Knock the ball down if you can't. Do your job, and we won't have to worry about the other team's piling up touchdowns against us."

Chip smiled to himself. Those were practically the same words Mr. Kash had spoken to the team. It looked like Phil was trying his best to imitate Mr. Kash in being a good coach.

So the team practiced hard on defense. And they practiced the new play, Play One.

Some of the players forgot which man they had to block. Phil and Mr. Quigley explained carefully again to them.

"It's a hard play," Chip said wonderingly. "Do you think we could do it in a game?"

"You're darn right you can," said Phil confidently. "All we have to do is work at it."

"No play is too tough if you keep working at it, Chip," added Mr. Quigley.

They sure sound like real coaches, thought Chip. He shrugged and went to his quarterback spot. They worked the play over and over again, and the team pulled it off better each time.

Occasionally they worked a simple play Mr. Kash had taught them, too. And they worked hard on improving their defense. But it was Play One that Coach Phil Wayne and Mr. Quigley concentrated on.

"Maybe Phil was holding out on us," Chip said to Splash as they walked away from the park after practice. "Maybe he really knows more about football than we thought he did."

"I don't know," said Splash, shaking his head. "I can't figure Phil out at all." Then he looked at Chip and asked, "Where were you last night, Chip? I mean, really?"

Chip had been expecting that question. "I felt all right," he said. "I wanted to quit football. But I changed my mind."

At two o'clock Saturday, the Stingrays, dressed in green-and-white uniforms, kicked off to the Cayugans, who were dressed in bright red-and-blue uniforms. The sun shone pale behind puffy white clouds, and a breeze was blowing, just enough to make playing comfortable.

The safety caught the boot and carried it up the field to the thirty-five. In the huddle, Chip called a play. The guys broke out and lined up at the line of scrimmage.

"Down!" Chip shouted. "One! Two! Hip!"

Chip caught the snap from the center, then handed it off to Spence, who charged with it through the line. He was hit on the thirty-six.

"A measly one-yard gain," Spence complained in the huddle. "Let me run it again, Chip."

"Okay. Firehose, Chazz, open up that hole for him."

They opened up a hole, and Spence went through for five yards. Then Chip tried a pass. It failed. Then they kicked. The Stingrays caught the punt on their ten and got as far as their twenty-two. They started to move the ball down the field. It appeared to be a move that couldn't be stopped.

It couldn't. The Stingrays bucked across for a touchdown and converted for a 7–0 lead.

In the second quarter, the Cayugans

managed to get to the Stingrays' twenty-yard line, the closest to the goal they'd been since the game had started.

Chip looked anxiously toward the sideline at Coach Phil Wayne. What was Phil waiting for? Why didn't he send in that play? Maybe he was waiting to pull it on the second down. Or the third.

Chip called for a line buck with Bill Perrett carrying the ball. Bill was a short, husky guy substituting for Spencer Keel. He lost a yard on the play and looked sick as he scrambled up from the bottom of the pile. Chip looked toward the sideline again. But Phil still wasn't sending in the play.

Chip tried a short pass. It was high. Tracy Tinker reached for it. It bounced off his hands and into the arms of a Stingray player! The Stingray buzzed off down the field and didn't stop until he had crossed the goal line.

Another touchdown! Chip gritted his teeth and shook his head.

The kick to convert was slightly to the right, leaving the score 13–0.

The Stingrays kicked off. The Cayugans caught the ball and carried it back to the twenty-eight before getting tackled. The Cayugans managed to get two first downs by the skin of their teeth. Both times the linesmen had to run onto the field with their chain and measure. And both times the nose of the ball just crossed the line by a couple of inches.

Chip started to name a play in the huddle when a sub burst in. "Hold it!" he said. "Phil wants Play One!"

Chip stared at him, then smiled with relief. "About time!" he said. "Okay, men! Let's go!"

There wasn't much time left on the clock. The ball was on the Stingrays' thirty-two yard line. The Cayugans hustled into position, Chip called signals, and the ball was snapped.

The play went off like a charm. Chip faked to Gordie, then tossed a lateral to Splash Tuttle. Splash circled around right end and went all the way.

The Cayugans' fans went crazy. They leaped and shouted, hardly believing what they'd seen. Spence booted for the extra point. It was good. 13–7.

In the third quarter, the Stingrays got hot again. As a matter of fact, they hadn't been cold at all. They rolled across the white ten-yard stripes slowly and sometimes swiftly. They were on the Cayugans' four-yard line when something happened. A fumble! The Cayugan safety scooped up the loose ball and dashed down the field to the Cayugans' twenty-four before he was tackled.

The Cayugans couldn't do much with it,

however. The ball was soon back in the Stingrays' possession. They had moved it down the field and gotten it to the Cayugans' nine when the third quarter ended.

The Stingrays' first play in the fourth was a pass. It worked beautifully — for the Cayugans, who intercepted it and bolted down the field to their thirty-eight. While the fans roared, the offense ran onto the field. Chip looked toward the sideline.

The play, Phil! he pleaded silently. *Send in the play!*

Phil was looking and pacing back and forth at the same time, as if wondering whether this was the time to send in the play or not. He didn't send it in.

Chip tried a run through right tackle and gained two yards. Luther Otis, another backfield sub, bucked for two more. And then in came a sub, running as fast as his legs could carry him.

"Firehose, take off!" he cried breathlessly. And to Chip, "Play One!"

Chip's heart soared. "About time!" he said. But what if it didn't work this time? They just might have been lucky that first time.

They pulled the play, and it worked *again!* Splash went all the way for a touchdown. Once more the Cayugans' fans went crazy! The Cayugans themselves jumped all over the place and slapped each other on the shoulders, taking so much time that the ref blew his whistle and reminded them that the game wasn't over yet.

The kick was good, and the Cayugans went into the lead 14–13.

Somehow the Cayugans kept the Sting-rays from putting across another touchdown, managing to win the game they had been so sure they were going to lose. When the team walked off the field, Phil Wayne was so pleased that he shook the hand of every member on the team. "Great game!" he kept saying. "Great game!"

Chip shook his hand, turned, and almost ran smack into Danny Livermore.

"Gosh, that was a great game, wasn't it, Chip?" Danny asked. "You really worked that new play! But I knew you'd be able to do it!" Danny clutched his notebook tightly and nodded, a wide grin on his face.

Chip was so happy that he couldn't help grinning back. "Yeah, we did okay today," he replied. "Thanks to that play of Phil's, that is. But can he come up with any more like that one?"

Danny's smile widened. "Oh, I'm sure he can. He's a great guy. Just like you, Chip!"

At Monday night's practice, Phil appeared more nervous than usual. Chip could hardly believe that the victory over the Stingrays could have affected the coach so much.

"Boys," Phil said, and cleared his throat. "Boys, I've got a new play we're going to start practicing this evening."

"A new one?" Chip's sun-browned face lit up. "A new play, Coach?"

"That's right. A new play." Phil cleared his throat again and looked at the notebook in his hand. "We're going to call it Play Two."

Chip frowned. "What about Play One, Coach? Are we going over that, too?"

Phil's blue eyes roved over to Chip. "We're going to forget Play One for a while, Chip," he said. "We're just going to concentrate on Play Two. Er . . . now, let's see. Get into position, boys. First team on offense, second team on defense. Help them out, will you, Mr. Quigley?"

Twenty-one players scrambled into position, then stood and looked at their head coach as he studied the notebook in his hand.

"This play isn't too hard to do," Phil promised. "If we work it right, it could get us out of a tough spot. Okay, listen: Toots snaps the ball to Chip. Chip fakes a handoff to Spence, and Spence runs toward the right side of the line, pretending he has the ball. At the same time, Splash runs toward the right side, too. Chip laterals the ball to him. Then Chip turns and runs toward the left sideline. Splash throws him a pass on the flat. That's all there is to it." He smiled. "Well, maybe there is a *little* bit more to it. We've got to have blocking, too. Hans, you run down the field straight at the defensive right halfback, and then cut right toward the center of the field. Marty, you pull out from left guard and block the right linebacker. Toots . . ."

One by one Phil explained to each player what he had to do. Then he repeated everything he'd said. The team worked on the play. Chip found that his job was easy.

They worked the play until everyone knew exactly what to do. Chip noticed Danny Livermore watching Phil Wayne with glowing eyes and a proud smile on his face. He sure admired Phil. Chip half hoped that Danny would start following Phil around instead of him.

The Cayugans practiced the play every day that week except Friday, their rest day.

On Saturday they tangled with the Duck-bills, who had won the week before, beating the Black Elks. There were only four teams in the league: the Cayugans, the Stingrays, the Duckbills, and the Black Elks.

All week long, the kids in school had seemed positive that the Duckbills would trim the Cayugans. The Duckbills had a clever quarterback, Nick Savino, and a tough fullback, Joe Bloom.

But what really tilted their opinion in favor of the Duckbills was the Cayugans them-selves. They were just lucky to have beaten the Stingrays, the crowd figured. Except for those two plays, the Cayugans had looked pretty lousy throughout the whole game. It was a good thing they had pulled off those plays at the right time, or they would have been skunked.

After the end of the first quarter, it appeared that the fans who had figured the Duckbills would smother the Cayugans had figured right. Nick Savino of the Duckbills flipped a short pass for a touchdown, then kicked for the extra point. It was good. Later he threw a long one. It would've gone for another touchdown if the intended receiver hadn't run into one of the goalposts.

In the second quarter, the Duckbills made some long successful runs. One of them resulted in a touchdown that didn't count because the referee spotted a Duckbill throwing a block from behind.

"Clipping!" yelled the referee.

Before the half was over, though, Joe Bloom broke through tackle for a twenty-four-yard touchdown run. The half ended with the Duckbills leading 14–0.

"We'd better start using Play Two this second half," Chip said to Phil. "We'd just better, or they'll trim us."

"Hang on, Chip," Phil said calmly. "We'll use it all right."

His voice was calm. But Chip saw that the hand holding the notebook was trembling.

The Cayugans pulled the big play just before the end of the third quarter. They had their backs against the wall — right on their own eight-yard line. Chip didn't figure that Phil would call in the play now, but he did.

It went off perfectly. Chip lateraled the ball to Splash. Splash heaved him a forward pass, which he caught and carried all the way down to the Duckbills' end zone. Spence converted for the extra point.

The Duckbills began rolling again. Twice the flag was dropped as the referee spotted

Duckbills linemen offside. The Duckbills sputtered about the calls and tried harder than ever to regain lost ground. Then they fumbled the ball on their twenty-two-yard line, and the Cayugans recovered.

"Chip!" said a new voice in the huddle. "Phil wants us to use Play Two!"

It was a substitute. Another player ran off the field.

Chip smiled. "Okay. Play Two. Let's go!"

This time, the play didn't click. Hans Lodder's man had gotten past him and was about to tackle Chip. Luckily, Chip managed to twist out of his grasp, got a nice block from Jim Kolar, and went galloping down the field for the Cayugans' second touchdown.

The kick for an extra point wasn't good, and Chip's spirits sank again. They trailed the Duckbills 14–13. A tie, at least, would've been better.

But the game wasn't over yet. In the fourth quarter, with two and a half minutes to go, Spence booted a field goal from the Duckbills' fourteen. It was good! The fans went wild again.

The game ended with the Duckbills on the Cayugans' four-yard line: Cayugans 16, Duckbills 14.

Once again the Cayugans jumped for joy, laughing and shouting. Danny Livermore joined in the hilarity.

Then Splash looked around for the coach. "Hey," he said, "where's Phil?"

Chip and the others looked around, too. Phil was nowhere in sight.

"Guess he's gone," said Chip. "How do you like that? He didn't even give us a chance to congratulate him."

Chip turned to Danny. "Did Phil say anything to you, Danny?" he asked.

The manager of the undefeated Cayugans looked at Chip with his mouth open and his large eyes staring perplexedly.

"Well, just before the game was over, he wanted me to put all the balls into the bag," Danny replied. "Then, right after the game, he took the ball that was used in the game, stuck it in the bag, and ran to his car as if his house was on fire. I don't know why he left so suddenly."

"Did you ask him?" Splash asked.

"Yes. I said, 'Why are you leaving so soon, Phil?' He said he had to get home."

"That's all he said?"

"That's all."

What was troubling Phil? Chip wondered. He wouldn't have run off so quickly, without even congratulating his team, if something wasn't troubling him, would he?

"It must've been something very important," Danny said. "He wouldn't run off for no good reason." His eyes brightened as he turned to Chip. "Chip, those catches you made were the sensational moments of the game!"

Chip smiled. "Thanks, Danny. But Splash deserves a lot of the credit. He threw those passes."

"I know. They were right on target, too." Danny turned to the left halfback, whose dark hair was matted down from sweat. "Just like they were supposed to be."

Chip, Splash, Spencer, and Danny started to walk home together. The boys discussed Phil and the plays he had used in their two games. No matter how you looked at it, it was those special plays that had won the games for the Cayugans. They were difficult plays — a lot more difficult than any of those Mr. Kash had taught them. Yet Phil and Mr. Quigley had drilled the Cayugans until they had learned the plays well enough to pull them off successfully.

"I think Phil's been holding out on us," said Chip. "I think he knows more about football than we figured. Or even Mr. Kash figured."

"I think he does, too," said Splash. "He probably figured out those plays himself. Boy, they worked beautifully."

"Why should he have held out on us?" Spencer asked wonderingly. "Why didn't he tell Mr. Kash about those plays?"

"Phil isn't that kind of guy," said Danny mildly. "He keeps a lot of things to himself. Maybe he thought he would've embarrassed Mr. Kash if he had suggested any plays to him."

"That could be," agreed Chip. "Phil wouldn't do a thing that might make a guy think he's awfully smart or something."

On Monday, Phil had a new play he taught the boys. He called it Play Three. Chip and the other guys thought it was odd to give the plays such simple names. The whole idea of learning a brand-new play each week seemed strange, too. Chip had never heard of a coach doing things the way Phil Wayne was doing them.

The crazy part of it was that the plays worked. That Saturday, the Cayugans played the Black Elks and came away with a win, 20–14. The second touchdown for the

Cayugans had been scored by accident. The Black Elks had fumbled a snap from center, which Gordie had recovered and had run all the way down the field with. But the first and third touchdowns were the results of the new play Phil Wayne had taught them.

The crowd, which had almost doubled since the first game, cheered their heads off when the game was over. All through the game, the Black Elks had looked so much better than the Cayugans that it had seemed impossible for them to lose. But lose they did. The Black Elks could hardly believe it themselves as they trudged off the field.

Chip saw Phil toss the last ball into the canvas bag and could tell that the coach was anxious to leave quickly again. But Phil was stopped by a short, gray-haired man with a stubble of beard. It was Jasper McFall, a grumpy-looking character but a real foot-ball fan.

"Say, Phil," he said, squinting at the coach with piercing brown eyes, "where'd you get that play that you used to pull off those touchdowns?"

Chip thought that Phil's face turned a shade pale. "Just got them, Jasper," Phil answered, his voice wavering a little. "Worked okay, didn't they?"

"They sure did. But I'm kind of curious, Phil," Jasper McFall said. Chip took a step closer so as not to miss anything. "We used that play sixty years ago at the high school when I was playing backfield. Saw your first two games and recognized the plays you used in them, too. We used them ourselves . . . sixty years ago. Where'd *you* get them, Phil?"

Phil's face turned a shade paler. All at once, without saying another word to Jasper McFall, he slung the bag of football equipment over his shoulder and strode away. This time Danny went along with him, one hand under the bag to make it lighter for the coach. Danny looked back once and gave Jasper McFall a dirty look.

"What about it, Mr. Quigley?" Jasper McFall asked the assistant coach. "Where did Phil get those tricky plays?"

Mr. Quigley shrugged. "I haven't the slightest idea, Mr. McFall. I thought they were his own."

"His own, nothing," Jasper snorted. "He couldn't dream up plays like that. You heard me say that we used those same plays sixty years ago, didn't you? Well, we did. He got them from somebody who played then, and I'm going to find out who!"

With that he gave another snort and tromped disgustedly away.

7

During the noon hour on Monday, Chip and Splash went to see Jack McKane, the high school football coach. Chip had known Mr. McKane for years, since he was a friend of Chip's father. Mr. McKane was six feet, four inches tall and thin as a rail. You'd think he'd been a basketball player back in his college days, but he hadn't. He had played end on his football team. There was something else that surprised a lot of people. He wrote short stories for boys' magazines.

He asked the boys to sit down, then looked at them across his broad, almost bare desk.

"Well, Chip, Splash, I'm honored by your visit." Mr. McKane smiled at them. "But neither of you is a student of mine, so it isn't because of poor marks, is it?"

Chip grinned. "No, it isn't, Mr. McKane." Then he explained about the new plays Phil had taught them and about the plays' helping the Cayugans win all of their games.

"We just want to know if you gave Phil those plays," said Chip. "He wouldn't say anything about them. And Jasper McFall said that his high school team had used them sixty years ago."

"Sixty years ago? And who's Jasper Mc-Fall?"

"An old guy who comes to all our football games," answered Chip. "He said that he used to play in the backfield for the high school."

Mr. McKane picked up a pencil and began tapping it against the desk. "No, I'm sorry, Chip. I'm not the one who's given any plays to your coach. Fact is, I don't even know Phil Wayne."

"Well . . . okay. Thanks, Mr. McKane."

The boys got up to leave. Mr. McKane swung around in his swivel chair. "Have you asked Bart Franks? He played football in college. Maybe he's the one."

"I don't think it would be him," said Splash. "His kid plays with the Stingrays."

Mr. McKane chuckled. "In that case, you're right. I don't think it'd be him, either." He rose from the chair and walked out into the hall with the boys. "Probably it wouldn't be anyone who went to college in recent years, anyway. If this Jasper McFall says his team used those plays sixty years ago, then it's probably someone who played on the team then. But what if someone did give the plays to your coach? Why should anyone care? There's nothing wrong in using old football plays."

Chip shrugged. "It really doesn't matter, I guess. It's just that Jasper McFall was so concerned about it. And why does Phil have to be so mysterious about it?"

"You have a point there. Maybe Phil has a good reason why he doesn't want anyone to know where he gets the plays. And you say he's been using a new one every week?"

"Yes. He might teach us a new one at our practice tonight, too. If he *has* a new one."

"Hmm, sounds interesting. Let me know how everything comes out."

"Sure will," said Chip.

Sure enough, Phil Wayne had a new play that evening. He called it Play Four. He explained it to the boys and Mr. Quigley, then the coaches helped the team work it. It was another clever play that was supposed to result in a touchdown if it went off right.

Of course nearly all plays are supposed to result in touchdowns, Phil Wayne reminded the boys. But these were special plays. He wanted the Cayugans to use a different one each week so that the opposing team would be caught completely off guard. They would continue using the new plays in each game, plus those Mr. Kash had taught them.

After practice, Chip and Danny were helping Phil with the equipment when a man came hobbling across the field. It was Jasper McFall again.

"Phil!" Jasper yelled before he was within twenty feet of the coach. "That's another play we used sixty years ago. Now don't tell me you dreamed that one up!"

A grin flickered on Phil's lips, then died.

"Okay, I suppose I have to confess sooner or later," he said. "Someone's been sending me those plays through the mail, Jasper."

Jasper McFall's eyes gazed steadily on the coach's as if he didn't dare blink for fear Phil Wayne would vanish from his sight. "Who?"

"I don't know," said Phil honestly.

"Horsefeathers!" Jasper McFall snorted. "Somebody who played with me during those days is giving you those plays. Now, who is it? Sakes alive, man, what harm is there in telling me? I just want to know, that's all. How about it, Mr. Quigley?"

"I don't know any more about it than Phil does," replied Mr. Quigley.

"I told you," said Phil seriously, "I don't know. Whoever sends those play patterns to me never signs his name."

"Blah!" Jasper McFall snorted again. "Young men nowadays are just too smart for their own good. Won't give you a decent answer." He stalked away angrily, grumbling under his breath.

Chip approached Phil. "Coach, is it really true that someone's been sending you the plays through the mail?"

Phil looked around cautiously. "You and Danny stick around until the others leave," he said quietly. "I'll tell you about it then."

"Can you tell Splash, too?" asked Chip. "He can keep a secret."

Phil considered it a moment. "Well, guess it won't hurt for Splash to know."

After all the other guys had gone, Phil repeated what he had said before. He had received the plays through the mail from someone who didn't sign his name. When the first play had come to him, he didn't know whether he should use it or not, since he didn't know who had sent it, or whether the play would help the Cayugans. His frank opinion was that since the Cayugans looked so poor in practice and since both he and Mr. Quigley were poor coaches, nothing they did would help them score touchdowns, let alone win games.

Then he discussed the strategy of Play One with Mr. Quigley, and they decided to teach it to the team. That was all they would have the team do for the whole week: learn the play until they had it down pat. If they won, fine. They would use it again the next week.

But what happened? A *new* play came to him through the mail! The first play had been a success, so Phil figured that the new one might be, too.

That was why they had kept using a new play every week. And each one had been working out perfectly.

"When do you get these plays?" Chip asked curiously.

"Every Monday," said Phil. "And I notice

that each time the envelope is stamped twelve P.M. Saturday."

"What kind of paper are the plays drawn on?"

"Looks like ordinary computer paper to me," answered Phil.

Chip's eyes widened. "Ordinary computer paper?"

"Yup."

Chip's brows wrinkled in thought. "If there were only a way to catch the person when he mails the letter," he said.

"Maybe we can watch the mailboxes and the post office," said Splash. "Catch the person red-handed."

"Hardly," said Phil. "Too many people in town we don't know."

Then how can we find out who the person is? thought Chip. There was no way. None at all.

✿   ✿   ✿

The Cayugans played the Stingrays that Saturday afternoon. It looked as if it was another game the Cayugans had no chance of winning. Quarterback Jack Stone for the Stingrays called play after play that gained a yard or two, sometimes five or ten. Once Jim Randall, their hot fullback, carried the ball for seventy-six yards for a touchdown.

Yet, when the game was over, the Cayugans were the winners. In the scorebook, the Stingrays had gained three times as many yards on runs and passes as the Cayugans had. But in the scoring column, it was the Cayugans who fared better, 18–14.

And it was the new play, Play Four, that had helped the Cayugans win.

On Monday, just before practice, Phil and Mr. Quigley were standing at the sidelines looking at a sheet of paper in Phil's hand. Phil motioned Chip and Danny over. "I received a new play again today," he said. "And the letter was stamped twelve o'clock Saturday."

It was another complicated play.

"I'm not sure whether we ought to keep learning these new plays," Phil said to Mr. Quigley undecidedly. "It bothers me to teach them and not know who's sending them."

Mr. Quigley shrugged. "Well, we're winning, aren't we?" he said, and chuckled.

"Sure," said Chip. "And as long as someone sends us the plays and we can learn them, let's use them."

Danny grinned. "That's the way I'd feel about it too," he said. "If somebody wants to help us, good for him!"

Halfway through their practice session, Chip looked over to the sidelines for Jasper McFall. The grumpy old man wasn't around.

Suddenly an idea occurred to him. After practice, while Chip and Splash were walking home together, Chip explained what he had in mind. "If Mr. McFall remembers those plays, maybe it's someone who played with him who's sending them to us. If he can remember those plays, he should remember who played with him, shouldn't he?"

"He should," agreed Splash.

They found Jasper McFall raking up leaves in his backyard.

"Well, well, look who's here!" the old man said. His eyes bounced from one boy to the other like Ping-Pong balls. "The Cayugan champions. The worst team in the league and winning all the games. I've never seen the likes of it in my seventy-five years. Come to help me rake up the leaves, did you?"

Chip smiled nervously. "We could, if you'd like," he said. "But we came for something else, Mr. McFall."

"I figured you did." A crooked smile broke over Mr. McFall's weathered face. "Something about those new plays?"

"Yes. We're trying to find out who's sending them to us. Since you said it's not you, we think it could be someone who played on the high school team when you did. Can you remember the names of the guys you played with, Mr. McFall?"

"Well, now, let me think." Mr. McFall scratched the stubble of beard on his chin. "Got a good memory, should be able to. The two halfbacks were Ken Strong and Mike Podack. Fullback was . . . let's see . . . Galloping Jim Fox."

Chip's eyes brightened. "Just a minute, Mr. McFall. Can you get a pencil and paper and write those names down for us?"

"Sure can," said Mr. McFall. Then he yelled toward the house, "Minnie! Bring out a paper and pencil!"

A moment later the back door opened and a woman wearing a blue apron over a yellow dress poked her head out. "What're you yelling your head off about, Jasper?"

"Bring me a paper and pencil!" Mr. McFall yelled again. "Us men've got something real important to talk about."

She disappeared into the house and returned with paper and pencil, grumbling about why didn't he go after them himself. While Mr. McFall named his football teammates, Chip wrote their names and the positions they had played. Mr. McFall named only those who had played regularly. There were a few, he admitted, whose names he couldn't remember.

The name of one player started Chip thinking. That was Oswald Kash, Coach Kash's father. He had played quarterback. Chip could hardly control his excitement as he thanked Mr. McFall and took off with Splash.

"I think we've got the answer, Splash," he said. "Remember what Phil said about the paper looking like ordinary computer paper? Bet it comes from Mr. Kash's company! Bet it's *him* who's been sending Phil the plays. He must've gotten them from his father."

"Why would *he* send them to him?"

"Because he wants him to have a winning team."

"How can we prove it was him?"

"We'll have to make him confess," Chip said.

"Confess? How are we going to make him do that?"

"Simple," said Chip. A smile broadened on his face. "I'll just call and ask him! But I think we've got this thing solved."

Chip and Splash hurried to Chip's house. Chip found Coach Kash's number and quickly dialed it. Coach Kash answered after two rings.

"This is Chip Chase," Chip said, hoping his voice wasn't wavering.

"Chip! This is a surprise. I've been following the team's record in the town's newspaper. Sounds like Phil Wayne has really honed your skills in the past weeks. He must have some secret weapon I didn't."

Chip cleared his throat. "Well, that's what I'm calling about, sir," he said. "Coach, someone is sending Phil plays in the mail every week. But he doesn't know who it is."

"Well, Chip, I'm sorry not to be able to help you, but it's not me." Chip could hear the surprise in Coach Kash's voice. "I've been keeping up with the team, but that's all I've had time for since starting this new job."

Chip was crestfallen. "Oh. Well, thanks."

"Just out of curiosity, why did you think it was me?"

Chip explained about the connection between Oswald Kash and Jasper McFall. Mr. Kash chuckled. "Ah, yes. I often wondered if Mr. McFall was coming to our games to watch you kids play — or to watch me coach so he could report back to Dad."

Chip suddenly had another idea. "Mr. Kash, do you think your dad could be the one sending in the plays?"

Mr. Kash was silent for a moment. Then

he said, "I'd be surprised if he was. I mean, why would he send them to a man he doesn't know and not to me, his own son, when I was coaching? But let me ask you this: What makes you so sure it's not Jasper McFall? He could be telling you it isn't him just to send up a smoke screen."

Chip hung up and turned to Splash with a thoughtful look.

"What?" Splash asked impatiently.

Chip told him what Mr. Kash had said about the smoke screen. Splash just shook his head. "It wouldn't make sense, would it? Why would the guy go to so much trouble? Why not just suggest the plays to Phil instead?"

Chip shrugged. "Maybe he thought Phil wouldn't use them. I mean they're sixty years old, after all."

Splash looked unconvinced. "A play's a

play, no matter how old it is," he said. "Our winning streak proves that."

"True." Chip slumped into a chair. Then suddenly he sat upright. "I know someone who might be able to help us figure this out. Who claims to know Phil Wayne better than anyone else on the team?"

With a snap of his fingers, Splash answered, "Danny Livermore! You're right! If he can't figure out this puzzle, no one can. Let's go."

The two boys hurried to Danny's house. They weren't the only ones there, though. To their amazement, there was a police car with its lights flashing parked in the driveway. Luther Otis was there, too. When he saw Chip and Splash, he hurried over.

"Danny's lost in the swamp!" he cried. "We were out there collecting leaves and stuff for our science project. Danny was going to show me how to set up something on my computer so my project would look really good. We got separated, and when I tried to find him, I couldn't!"

Just then the police officer called over to them: "We have a search party ready to go look. We'll need you to come with us, Luther, to show us where you last saw him."

"Can we come, too?" Chip asked. "He's our team manager, and we'd like to help find him!"

The officer studied them, glanced at the sky, then nodded. "It's still early enough so it won't get dark. Just stick together when you're out there, and always keep an adult in sight. One lost boy is enough for one day."

Chip, Splash, Luther, and Mr. and Mrs. Livermore piled into the Livermores' car. They followed the police car out to the conservation area parking lot. The swamp was deep inside the park's boundaries. A crew of other people, mostly adults, was already there. At a word from the police officer, they set out to search for Danny.

Luther took the lead through the tangled brush. Over their heads loomed giant trees, their brown and yellow leaves whispering in the gently blowing breeze. Birds scurried from branches with a wild flutter of wings. The searchers ran on, now and then their clothing snagging or their arms being scratched by the barbs of a bush.

Danny's been out here a long time! Chip's mind screamed. Maybe we'll be too late!

Presently Luther slowed his pace, paused, and stared around in confusion.

"What's the matter, Luther?" Chip cried. "You didn't forget where you last saw him, did you?"

"I — I thought it was near here," murmured Luther, his face as pale as one of the yellow leaves.

Chip forgot that Danny had ever bothered him. He hated thinking of the little guy being stuck out here, scared and alone for hours. He cupped his hands to his mouth. "Danny!" he yelled.

The last whisper of sound died behind them as the searchers stopped in their tracks. They listened silently for an answer. All they heard was the soft mocking murmur of the leaves.

A lump lodged in Chip's throat. Danny Livermore was an egghead, but he wasn't a bad kid. He wasn't a bad kid at all.

"Danny!" Chip yelled again. "Danny, yell out if you hear me!"

And then, from somewhere to their left they heard a voice! "He . . . re! He . . . re!"

A cry burst from Chip's throat. He plunged through the woods, ignoring the barbs that clawed at him. He knew, as many others did, about the patches of swampland. It was especially soft and dangerous after a heavy rain. Here and there, signs that read BE-WARE: SWAMP had been tacked onto trees. The signs were many years old, torn and ugly from the battering of rain, sleet, and snow. Was it because of their age that they had sometimes been ignored — as Danny may have ignored them?

Stumbling over a log, Chip went sprawling on his stomach. He scrambled to his feet, ran on, the leaves wet and soggy under his feet. He came upon a mammoth tree.

"The other side of that tree!" Luther cried. "I remember now!"

Chip led the way around it. Just ahead was a small clearing. Practically in the middle of it was Danny, buried in some kind of mud right up to his knees! He was clinging to a small branch of a tree. It had split where it was joined to a trunk.

"Did you bring a rope?" Chip's eyes were wide with concern.

"No. Didn't think of it," one of the men answered.

"Can we use our belts?"

"Guess we'll have to," the man said.

He took off his belt, and Chip started to take his off, but another man offered his belt first. It was longer and stronger, he said.

The men linked the two belts together and tossed one end to Danny. Danny caught it.

"Hold on tight!" one of the men said. "We'll pull you out!"

Danny's face was strained as he clung hard to the belt. The men pulled. Gradually Danny came oozing out of the mire. Chip and one of the men helped him onto solid ground. His clothes were a mess.

"Thanks!" he said, panting hard. "Thanks a million!"

And then he looked around, his eyes suddenly filled with horror. "My notebook!" he cried. "Where's my notebook?"

"Is that it?" Chip said, pointing. It was about two feet from where Danny had been trapped. One of the men got a long branch and poked the notebook up onto the ground. Chip started for it, but Danny bounded ahead of him, his legs covered with mud.

"I'll get it!" he said.

He picked up the notebook and opened it carefully. The anxiety on his face disappeared. There, among pages filed with writing and diagrams, was an assortment of brown, yellow, and red leaves, all of different shapes and sizes.

Danny smiled happily. He had not lost his prized treasure.

The search party returned to town. Danny squeezed into the backseat of his parents' car with Luther, Chip, and Splash. The Livermores dropped Luther off first.

Luther got out, then, holding the car door open, leaned back in. "Hey, Danny, do you think I should take my leaves now?"

Danny clutched his notebook protectively. "Why don't you come over tomorrow and get them?" he said. "That way we can work out a computer program for you at the same time."

Luther shrugged, then nodded and closed the door.

Chip was anxious to ask Danny about his thoughts on who the mystery play sender was. But he figured Danny was too exhausted from having been stranded in the mud for so long to talk about much. When Danny fell asleep after they'd dropped Splash off, he knew he had been right.

Danny slumped to one side, his mouth slightly open. His arms relaxed, and the notebook he'd been hugging to his chest slid out from between them. Before Chip could catch it, it fell to the floor and the leaves Danny and Luther had collected flew out. Chip carefully picked them up and tried to tuck them back in place.

Danny woke with a start. "What are you doing with my notebook?" he asked. He sounded angry. Chip looked at him in surprise.

"I was just putting these back in," he explained, handing Danny the notebook and fistful of leaves. "Here, you can do it if you want. I didn't know they went in a special place."

"Oh. Sorry," Danny apologized. "It's just that, well, I put some personal stuff in here, and I don't like people looking at it. You know . . . ," he finished lamely.

"Sure," Chip said. But he didn't really understand. What kind of "personal stuff" could a kid like Danny have?

"These leaves are pretty cool, though," Danny piped up. "You wanna see them?"

"Uh, okay," Chip replied. He wasn't all that interested, but he decided that if Danny wanted to show off his leaves, he wouldn't stop him.

"See this star-shaped one?" said Danny. "It's a sweet gum leaf. And these red ones are dogwood and scarlet oak. You ever collect leaves?"

"When I was younger I did." Chip secretly

thought that collecting leaves was a waste of time. But soon he found himself absorbed in the many leaves Danny pulled from his notebook. There was a fat oval magnolia leaf, a narrow oval elm, a bristle-tipped white oak, a saw-edged birch, and a cherry leaf that had a saw edge, too. The birch leaf was deep yellow.

"What do you collect leaves for, Danny?" Chip asked curiously.

"I collect all kinds of things, actually. I guess I just like learning, and sometimes reading about stuff isn't enough. If I see it for real, then it sticks with me better. That's why I'm managing the Cayugans, I suppose. Otherwise, I don't think I would have ever seen —" Danny stopped abruptly.

"Ever seen what?" Chip prodded.

"Oh, nothing. Ever seen a game close up, I guess."

The car pulled up to Chip's house, and Chip got out amid thank-yous from Mr. and Mrs. Livermore and Danny. He waved good-bye and watched the car pull away with a thoughtful expression on his face.

Chip wanted to sleep late Saturday morning, but his mom woke him up early.

"You and your dad are going to get haircuts this morning," she said. "Your hair is getting so long, it's beginning to cover your shoulders."

"Oh, Mom, it's not that bad," said Chip. She was always exaggerating.

He had an egg, a few strips of bacon, and milk for breakfast. Then he and his dad put on sweaters, coats, and hats, and bucked the strong wind that had started sometime during the night. They walked uptown to a barbershop — MOBY THE BARBER — the same man Mr. Chase had been going to for years.

Moby had another barber working with him, but Chip's dad always had Moby cut his hair. Moby knew exactly how Mr. Chase wanted it cut. As for Chip, he didn't care which barber cut his.

"Found out yet who's been sending those football plays?" Mr. Chase asked.

"Not yet," said Chip.

"Sure is funny," said his dad.

"Sure is," admitted Chip.

They reached the barbershop. There was a man already there, sitting in Moby's chair. Jim, the other barber, was reading a newspaper. He got up as they entered, said "Good morning," and brushed off the chair. Chip took off his coat and hat and sat down.

Moby finished cutting his previous customer's hair and started on Mr. Chase. They began talking about some professional football teams, and Chip figured that was another reason why his dad liked to sit in Moby's chair — so they could talk about football.

Chip's haircut was soon over, and he went to a chair near the wall to wait for his father. Even though it was half an hour before lunch, Chip was hungry. To take his mind off it, he gazed out of the window and watched the people stroll by. All at once he recognized a familiar figure walking on the sidewalk across the street. It was Jasper Mc-Fall. He walked up the street to the post office, entered it, and a minute later came back out.

Chip was filled with excitement. He pushed himself erect and stared at Jasper McFall until the old man had passed the window.

Was Mr. Kash right? Was Mr. McFall the person who was mailing Phil the plays?

Chip suddenly thought of a way he could test Mr. McFall. He slipped on his jacket and hurried up the street after the old man.

"Mr. McFall! Wait!" he called.

The old man stopped and turned. "Yes, what is it?" he asked gruffly.

"I wondered if you could help me," Chip said breathlessly. "I want to mail something to Phil Wayne, but I don't have his address. I thought maybe you might have it. Do you?"

Mr. McFall narrowed his eyes. "Why on earth would I have his address? As far as I'm concerned, he's nothing but a play-stealing sham of a coach!" With that, he spun on his heel and stormed off.

Chip was stunned. He stood staring after Mr. McFall for a moment, then felt a light tap on his shoulder. It was his father.

"What was that all about?" he asked.

Chip shook his head. "I wish I knew!" he said wonderingly. He explained to his father about Mr. Kash's suspicion that Mr. McFall was the secret play maker. "But I guess he's not," Chip added. "I don't know who it could be."

"Maybe a good hot meal will get your brain going better," Mr. Chase said. "Come on, I know I'm ready for lunch!"

"Okay," Chip agreed. A strong cold breeze fluttered his hair. "Oh, wait, Dad, I forgot my hat back in the barbershop!"

He ran down the block and was about to pass the post office when he collided with someone. He and the other person both fell on their backsides.

"Whoa, sorry, are you okay?" Chip said as he sat up. "Hey, Danny, is that you?"

It was Danny. But Chip wasn't looking at him. A movement beside Danny had caught his eye. It was Danny's notebook, open and flapping in the wind. But when Chip looked closer, he was sure the writing in the book wasn't Danny's. Or was it? On one page it looked like Danny's neat handwriting; on another the writing looked cramped and was broken up by strange symbols. Even the paper looked different. Chip suddenly realized that the odd pages were actually pieces of paper taped into the pages of Danny's notebook. There was something familiar about the strange pages, but before he could figure out what, Danny snatched up his book.

"Uh, hi, Chip. I'd like to stay and talk, but I've got to get going," Danny said hurriedly. A moment later, he disappeared down the street.

Chip shook his head, got his hat from the barbershop, and caught up with his father. The whole walk home he tried to puzzle out why the writing in Danny's notebook had looked familiar.

Then he figured it out.

"Hey, Dad," he asked, hardly able to restrain his excitement. "Do you have any books about football at home?"

When they got home, Mr. Chase found the book Chip was looking for. And inside it, Chip found what he was looking for. But he decided not to do anything with his information until he could be one hundred percent absolutely sure.

All week long, he stayed quiet. Phil had another new play to teach them at football practice, so he was busy both during school and after. But that was okay. He only needed to be free one day that week — Saturday, noontime.

✧   ✧   ✧

When that day finally arrived, Chip bundled himself up tight, pulled his hat over his eyes, and headed for the downtown area. But he wasn't getting another haircut. He was going to the post office.

It was quarter to twelve when he arrived. He settled himself into a chair behind a trash can. He didn't have to wait long.

Although the post office was a busy place on Saturday, he picked out the person he was waiting for in a second. The notebook he was carrying was a dead giveaway. So was the big envelope.

Chip waited until Danny was in line, then sidled up beside him.

"Hi, Danny! What do you have there?" he asked.

Danny jumped, then tried to hide the envelope behind his back. "N-nothing," he stammered. His face turned as red as a strawberry. "I mean, it's just a letter. M — my mother . . ." He paused, blinked, and looked at Chip.

Chip raised his eyebrows. "Can I see it, Danny?" he asked quietly.

Reluctantly, Danny brought the envelope from behind his back. He showed it to Chip. As Chip had suspected, it was addressed to Phil Wayne.

"There's a football play in here, isn't there?" Chip asked.

Danny nodded. He looked as guilty as if he had been caught red-handed stealing a million dollars.

"Unbelievable," Chip said, shaking his head. "You were the last person I suspected of sending the plays to Phil. If I hadn't seen your notebook last week, I bet it would still be a secret. Can I ask you something, Danny?"

Danny nodded.

"Why did you send the plays to Phil? Why not just give them to him?"

Danny snorted. "Do you really think he would have used them if I had, Chip?" he replied. "He would have asked me where I got them. Then he would have found out they were sixty years old."

"Where did you get them?" Chip asked.

"It was an accident, really. I went to a garage sale with my mom right after football season began. While she poked around through some stuff, I looked through a box of old books. I found an old playbook stuck in with them and bought it for a quarter. I kind of forgot about it until Coach Kash announced that Phil Wayne was taking over the coaching position. From the looks on everyone's faces, including Phil's, I knew we were in for a losing season unless a miracle happened. That's when I remembered the playbook."

Chip nodded with understanding. "So you copied the plays and sent them, one by one, to Phil."

"Yeah. I tore out the ones that I'd sent and stuck them in my notebook so I wouldn't send the same play twice." He showed Chip the pages. They were the ones Chip had glimpsed the previous Saturday.

"So tell me, whose garage sale was it you went to, Danny?"

Danny grinned. "You won't believe it — Jasper McFall's! His wife was running the sale, so I'm sure he doesn't even know she sold it."

Chip burst out laughing. "I wonder how Mr. McFall is going to feel when he learns he's been accusing Phil of stealing something his wife sold for a quarter!"

Then he tapped the envelope Danny was holding. "What should we do with that?" he asked.

Danny thought for a moment. " I guess it's time to confess," he said. "Let's take it to Phil, then to Mr. McFall. I just hope Phil doesn't boot me as manager."

The boys walked toward Phil Wayne's neighborhood, which was only a few blocks away. On the way, Chip tried to convince Danny that Phil would understand. But he wasn't so sure. After all, it's a little embarrassing to have a ten-year-old kid feeding you plays — and sixty-year-old plays at that.

Phil opened the door to Chip's knock.

"Well, good morning!" he greeted the boys jovially. "You must have something important to tell me that couldn't wait until practice on Monday. What's up?"

"We have news, all right," Chip replied. "You'll never guess who's been sending you those plays, Phil."

Phil looked from Chip to Danny. The look on Danny's face must have been a dead giveaway, because Phil's eyes grew wide with disbelief.

"You, Danny?"

"Yes." Danny nodded, blushing. He told him the whole story about how he came across the playbook. "I'm sorry I didn't tell you sooner. I — I was just trying to help the team, Phil. I only wanted to send you that first play to see what happened. But then, after it helped us win, I sent you another. And it helped us win, too. So . . ."

"So you just kept going." Phil scratched his head, then smiled. "Well, I hope I'm man enough to admit when I need help. And believe me, I'd rather be the coach of a winning team than a losing one! So there's nothing to be sorry about — except maybe for mystifying us for so long."

"Coach," Chip said. "Do you think you could come with us to Jasper McFall's house? Danny wants to tell him, too."

"And return his playbook."

Phil agreed. "I wouldn't miss it for anything," he said with a sparkle in his eye.

The threesome stopped at Danny's house first so he could retrieve the playbook, then drove to Mr. McFall's house in Phil's car. Jasper McFall answered on the first knock. When he saw who was there, he frowned.

"Yes, what is it?" he grumbled.

Danny stepped forward and handed him the playbook. "I think this belongs to you," he said.

Mr. McFall's eyebrows shot up. "My playbook!" he exclaimed. "Where did you get that? I've been looking for it ever since I first recognized the play this man stole from my old team!"

But before any of them could say a word, Mrs. McFall came to the door. "*That's* what you've been tearing the house apart looking for?" She sniffed. "I sold that old dusty thing weeks ago. To this young man, I believe. For a quarter." She smiled at Danny while her husband sputtered.

"A *quarter?* Why, any fool could have seen this book was worth its weight in gold! How could you have —"

"Oh, hush." Mrs. McFall dismissed him with a wave of her hand. "You haven't thought about that playbook for years. Besides, I would think you'd be pleased to know it came in so handy! After all, it did turn out a winning team, didn't it?"

Mr. McFall pondered that. "Hmm. When you put it like that, it doesn't sound so bad. Just makes me wish I'd thought of dragging these old plays out myself." He suddenly laughed. "But who knew they'd actually work still?"

"So we can keep using them?" Chip asked eagerly.

"You want to keep winning, don't you?" the old man demanded, a twinkle in his eye.

All three nodded enthusiastically.

"Well, then! Keep using 'em! And Phil, I owe you an apology. If there's anything I can do to make up for it . . ."

Phil cleared his throat. "Well, as a matter of fact, there is. Seems Adam Quigley isn't going to be able to assist me for the last few games of the season. I wonder if you would like to take over the job."

"Sir, you've got yourself a deal!"

Phil smiled mischievously. "Then you better get yourself dressed and ready to go. The game starts in an hour!"

"Holy cow!" Chip exclaimed. "I totally forgot!"

Phil rolled his eyes. "And this is our quarterback. See what I've had to put up with all season?" He punched Chip playfully in the shoulder. "Come on, let's get you home and suited up. We've got a new play to try out against those Duckbills!"

That afternoon the Cayugans tangled with the Duckbills. And, as everyone expected, they won again. The score was 19–14. The Duckbills had won only one game so far. They had split with the Black Elks.

After that day's game, the standings were as follows:

	Won	Lost
Cayugans	5	0
Stingrays	3	2
Black Elks	1	4
Duckbills	1	4

The Cayugans were in first place. Even if they lost the game next week, their last of the season, they would still be in first place.

Only one important question remained: Could they go through the entire season without a single loss?

Danny had given the envelope with the new play in it to Phil Saturday morning. On Monday evening at practice, Phil explained to the team about Danny's getting the football plays from Mr. McFall's old book and secretly mailing them to him every week. He also explained why Danny had done it.

Danny's face turned a deep red as all the guys looked at him. They were stunned with surprise. But happy, too.

"I'd say Danny deserves a round of applause, wouldn't you?" Phil said.

The response was thunderous. "Yea, Danny!" the guys shouted.

"I have a new play from Mr. McFall's

book again today," Phil said. "But I've decided not to use it."

The team was silent.

"Why not?" someone finally asked. "We want to keep winning, don't we, Phil?"

"Oh, I think we will," Phil replied. "We will be working out a new play today. But it's a brand-new play, not a sixty-year-old one. And for that, we have Mr. McFall, our new assistant coach, to thank. He and I spent hours looking through his old playbook. Then, in less than fifteen minutes, he sat down and drew out a whole new play. If I'm not careful, I'm going to be out of a job."

The boys all laughed, and Mr. McFall stepped forward with a smile on his face.

"No, thanks," he said. "Assistant coach is good enough for me! You see, the thing is, you fellows have been winning games for two reasons. Sure, the old plays helped a lot. But you've also improved as a team. Constant practice in blocking and passing while learning those hard plays has done the trick. Coach Wayne has done a great job working you boys into shape."

Phil Wayne added, "I don't think we have to depend on an exceptional play to help us score. In fact, I'd be willing to bet that we could win the game with the simple plays Mr. Kash devised. But since we do have this new one in hand, what do you say we give it a whirl?"

The boys cheered.

"Okay, then let's get going! We'll start by reviewing the basics. First team, line up in front of me. Second team, in front of Mr. McFall. Danny, hand me a ball, would you please?"

Like a drill team the boys hustled into position. Danny wrestled a ball from the equipment bag. Phil placed it on the ground.

"This is our line of scrimmage," he said.

"First team's ball. Regular T formation. Chip, call for Forty-two. Remember that one, Spence? You run the ball through tackle. Let's go."

The Black Elks won the toss the next Saturday afternoon, and chose to receive. Spencer Keel kicked off for the Cayugans. The ball sailed end over end across the white stripes, was caught on the twenty-five, and carried up to the Black Elks' thirty-four.

Chip was worried. Although the Black Elks had won only one game this season, it was possible for them to beat the Cayugans today. What if Jasper McFall's new play didn't work? It was the last game of the season, wasn't it? What harm was there in using one more sixty-year-old play?

But Phil figured that the Cayugans could win by using those easy plays Mr. Kash had taught them, plus the new ones they had learned. After all, the new plays had helped the Cayugans to five victories, hadn't they? Then, if they needed Mr. McFall's new play, they'd use it, too.

The Black Elks moved. Their fullback, Dick Clark, busted through left tackle for a six-yard gain. Then Bill Nelson charged through center on a quarterback sneak for a first down.

They ran hard. They fumbled. They recovered. They tried passes, which the Cayugans' backfield men knocked down. Once . . . twice . . . the referee's whistle shrilled. Two offside penalties in succession. The Black Elks were anxious. Too anxious. Or were they making mistakes because they were afraid of the Cayugans? Was that it? thought Chip. Were they really afraid that we might swamp them?

"Pass to Jim!" Chip said in the huddle as the Cayugans took the ball on their own eighteen.

It was a long, wobbly pass. Chip stared. Not far enough. It was intercepted!

The Black Elks player ran hard with it, while the crowd in the bleachers cheered. Then, on the Cayugans' four-yard line, Gordie Poole brought the runner down.

Hold that line! Hold that line!" yelled the Cayugans fans.

"Close in tight!" Chip ordered. "Don't let 'em get through!"

The Cayugans were in their 6-2-2-1 defense position, the linebackers hugging close to the linemen.

The Black Elks' quarterback, Bill Nelson, called signals. The ball snapped from center. Bill handed off to fullback Dick Clark. Dick smashed into the line.

Rubber cleats chewed the earth. Helmets and shoulder pads clattered as the blue-uniformed Black Elks charged against the red-and-blue Cayugans. A pileup formed. The whistle shrilled.

A one-yard gain.

"Hold them!" Chip yelled from the sidelines. "You've got to hold them!"

This time Bill Nelson tried his trick again, the quarterback sneak. Again a one-yard gain!

"All right!" shouted Chip. They had to hold those Black Elks. They just had to.

Bill called signals again, took the snap, then faded back to pass. He shot a quick one toward the right, barely over left end Hans Lodder's head. Splash, playing linebacker at that side, plunged forward and knocked the pass down.

"Nice going, Splash!" Chip cried.

Fourth down. The Black Elks' last chance to score. Will they try another pass? Will they try a line buck? Or will they try for a field goal? Chip's heart pounded as he waited to see what they would do.

They were going to try for a field goal! Bill Nelson was playing deep, Dick Clark several feet behind him.

Dick kicked. It was good! Three points for the Black Elks!

In the second quarter, the Black Elks almost scored again when they attempted a field goal from the eight-yard line. The ball missed sailing between the uprights by inches.

Between halves Danny ran out with a paper carton loaded with small cups of lemon-and-orange-juice mix. As he handed Chip his, a smile curled his lips.

"You guys look great, Chip," he said quietly. "Even better than before, I think."

"Thanks, Danny." Chip watched him passing cups to the other players and thought, What a guy. Who could ever believe that a team that had been destined to lose every game would win five straight? Perhaps six straight, if they were lucky and won today. And all because of a little guy, a kid who collected stuff.

Coach Phil Wayne made some substitutions in the second half. Chip feared that the substitutes might make them lose the game. Some of them were poor players. Still Phil played them. It was a rule in the league. Every player on each team had to play at least two minutes in a game.

The Black Elks kicked off to the Cayugans to start off the second half. The Cayugans caught the ball and carried it to their twenty-nine. Chip worked it across the forty to the Black Elks' thirty-one. Twice Spence bucked the line for seven- and five-yard gains.

On the Black Elks' eighteen, they were stopped. They couldn't gain an inch. The

Black Elks' line held like a cement wall. Chip tried a pass on the third down. It was knocked down. Then they tried a field goal. The ball missed the uprights by four feet.

Once again the Black Elks moved forward. But they moved slowly. Now and then one of their linemen was called on an offside penalty charge, which cost them five yards. Another time a Black Elk hit a Cayugan from behind. "Clipping!" yelled the referee.

The Black Elks were forced to punt from their twenty-two-yard line. The ball wobbled lazily through the air and dropped into Luther Otis's hands. Luther had replaced Splash in the backfield. Nestling the ball against his chest, he ran down the sideline to the Cayugans' twenty-nine, where he was smeared.

The referee carried the ball in a third of the width of the field. The Cayugans tried a line buck that went for a two-yard gain, then Chip heaved a long pass to right end Tracy Tinker.

It was intercepted!

The Black Elks' runner went twenty yards before he was brought down. The whistle shrilled, ending the third quarter.

The Black Elks moved the ball slowly toward the Cayugans' goal line, and their fans in the stands began to chant, "We want a touchdown! We want a touchdown!" And they stamped their feet on the bleachers.

Chip sweated. Time sped swiftly. The Black Elks seemed headed for a touchdown to satisfy their hungry fans. If they got one, would the Cayugans be able to come back and win? If the Cayugans had had a tried-and-true play up their sleeves, Chip wouldn't have worried so much. But they had only a brand-new play to rely on.

The ball was on the Cayugans' eleven-yard-line. The Black Elks tried a pass. It sailed deep into the right-hand corner of the end zone. Chip felt his heart sink as he saw the Black Elks receiver reach for it.

And then Gordie Poole leaped and knocked it down!

"Nice going, Gordie!" Chip shouted, jumping up and down on the sidelines.

The Black Elks tried an end-around run. It went for three yards. They tried another pass, a short one over center.

Gordie intercepted it! He ran toward the right side of the field but was smeared on the eighteen. Chip thumped him on the back as he passed him on the field.

The Cayugans moved the ball forward slowly, gained a first down by two inches. Hardly fast enough. They called time and rested. Chip thought of the play they had used last week to beat the Duckbills. He mentioned it to Phil. They tried it and gained three yards. It seemed that the Black Elks could stop them no matter what play the Cayugans used.

Finally Phil sent in for Mr. McFall's new play. It was an end-around run, with Splash following close behind Chip. Chip went over the play in the huddle. Time-in was called. The players got into their positions.

"Down! One! Two! Three! Hip!" barked Chip.

He took the snap and dashed toward left end. Jim Kolar and Hans Lodder blocked their men. Then Hans ran ahead to block the deep linebacker, while behind him raced Chip, the ball nestled in the crook of his arm.

A Black Elks defenseman reached for him. Chip tossed a lateral to Splash, then turned and blocked the oncoming Black Elk. Splash ran hard up the field. A few steps behind him was Spence, who had swung to his left when the play had begun. A Black Elks linebacker got by Hans and reached for Splash. Splash tossed a lateral to Spence.

"Go, Spence, go!" shouted Chip.

Spence went — all the way down the field to the Black Elks' goal! A touchdown! The place kicker kicked for the extra point, and it was good.

The Black Elks couldn't catch up. The Cayugans won 7–3.

After the handshaking with the Black Elks was over, after all the cheering and the shouting, Phil thanked the Cayugans. Especially one person whom he pulled toward him and shook hands with. Danny Livermore.

"Here's the boy we owe our successful season to," Phil said. "Danny Livermore, our manager. If it weren't for his sending us the plays Mr. McFall's team used sixty years ago, we really might've had a season of defeats instead of six straight victories. Let's give Danny a great big hand."

The guys yelled and applauded for Danny.

Chip applauded the loudest of all. To think I almost quit this team, he thought with a smile. And if it weren't for this little guy, I would have. Just goes to show — you really can't judge a book by its cover. Unless it's an old playbook, that is!

READ ALL THE BOOKS

In The

New MATT CHRISTOPHER Sports Library!